# The Day Hans Got His Way

## A NORWEGIAN FOLKTALE

*Retold by* David Lewis Atwell    *Illustrated by* Debby Atwell

HOUGHTON MIFFLIN COMPANY

BOSTON 1992

**Library of Congress Cataloging-in-Publication Data**

Atwell, David Lewis.

    The day Hans got his way : a Norwegian folktale / retold by David Lewis Atwell :
illustrated by Debby Atwell.

      p.  cm.

    Summary: Convinced that his work in the field is harder than his wife's work at home, a
farmer trades places with her for the day.

    ISBN 0-395-58772-7

    [1. Folklore — Norway.]   I. Atwell, Debby, ill.   II. Title.

PZ8.1.A85Day   1992

398.2 — dc20

[E]                                    91-43945

                                              CIP

                                              AC

Printed in the United States of America

HOR 10 9 8 7 6 5 4 3 2 1

We would like to express our admiration and gratitude to the memory of Peter Christen Asbjornsen and Jorgen Moe whose love of story and the spoken word led them to traverse the Norwegian countryside collecting and preserving folktales of the Norse community. Thanks to their original efforts a century and a half ago, we are able today to maintain a precious link to our collective past.

D.A.

Now, some men are master carpenters and some men master cobblers. Hans was a master complainer. Oh yes, Hans knew complaining, for by his reckoning no one could do anything as well as he. Nothing ever pleased him. And true to the grumbler's call, if fault could be found he most certainly would find it.

So it was that one evening, with finger pointed as ever at his kind and hardworking wife Gertrude, Hans complained, "It's not fair that I have to cut hay all day in the hot sun while you laze about here. Tomorrow you should go to work in the fields and I will mind the house."

The next morning, wishing to be at peace with her husband, Gertrude agreed to give him his way.

Oh, how Hans smiled at the idea of so easy a day's labor. At last he would show his wife how a house should be run.

So Gertrude, with scythe in hand, bid Hans a good day.

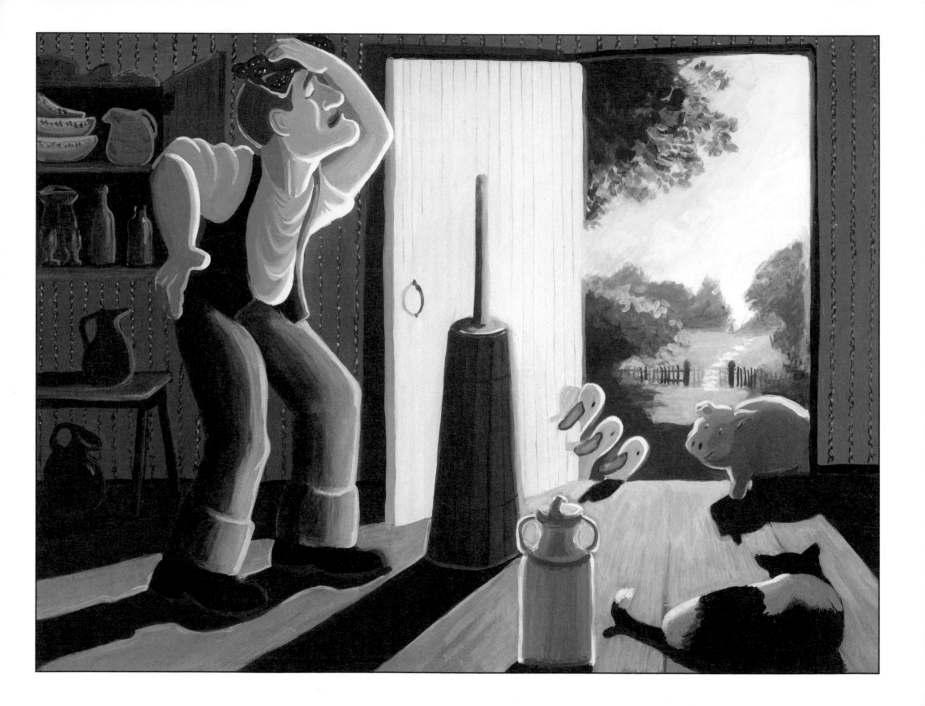

At once Hans began to look around for some simple task. Well, as meat loves salt, Hans loved butter. So he fetched a gallon of fresh cream from the larder and poured it carefully into the churn. He churned and churned, and the more he churned the harder was the churning, for it takes stout arms to churn cream into butter.

"Something must be wrong with this churn," Hans muttered. "It can't be made properly. I should have built it myself!" But in spite of the unsatisfactory churn he kept at it, growing hotter and wearier all the while, until finally his thoughts turned to the cool barrel of cider down in the cellar.

He put aside the churn and climbed down the cellar stairs. Oh, how good this cool, sweet cider is going to taste, he thought, as he knelt with tap and mallet in hand before the wooden keg.

Just as he gave the tap a solid whack, there came a frightful commotion from above.

"Good grief!" bellowed Hans, and he charged up the stairs to have a look.

There he found the butter churn overturned and Hamlet the family pig greedily slopping up the thick sweet cream. At the sight of this, Hans's face turned bright red, and with mallet raised he made for the poor creature with such fury that it jumped straight up into the air and raced out the door.

As Hans stood blustering at the fleeing pig, he suddenly realized that he was still holding in his hands not only the mallet but also the tap that was meant for the keg.

"Oh, no," Hans groaned. "No. No. No."

With little thought and all haste, Hans made for the cellar. But when his feet struck the slick cream-covered floor — away he went. Bumpity bumpity bumpity bump! Down the cellar stairs he tumbled, landing at the bottom with a splash. And there he sat, soaking but safe in a sea of cider.

But not for long. While the last of the cider dripped from the keg, a flurry of hysterical quacking erupted from the top of the stairs. "Now what?" Hans shrieked, storming up the stairs yet again.

It was not long, though, before he looked up from his labor to see Elsa the cow. "Oh, rotten rutabagas," Hans grumbled, remembering that it was well past time for her watering.

"All right, all right," Hans said to the cow. "Just a moment." He was determined that nothing further should happen to the churn and its precious contents, so he strapped it to his back. Smiling with pride at his foresight, Hans set off with Elsa for the well.

When he arrived at the well, Elsa began to moo expectantly. Hans, too, was more than eager for the taste of some fresh well water, since he had been deprived of his cider.

And so, forgetting the butter churn strapped to his back, Hans leaned headlong over the well to fetch the bucket. When he did, all the cream from the churn spilled out into the well.

"What am I to do? Now there is no butter for supper, our cider is gone, and the well will be sour for months!" Hans howled. Elsa only mooed. "It's getting late, and I haven't made the porridge, and there certainly isn't time to take you all the way to pasture." Hans sat shaking his head.

At last he had an idea. Ha! He would graze the cow on the sod roof atop the house. Some fine grass grew there, and, as the house was built into the hillside, he had little trouble getting Elsa up on the roof. And he could still show Gertrude how to prepare a timely supper.

But first, to be sure Elsa wouldn't fall off the roof, Hans tied a rope around her neck. Next he dropped the other end of the rope down the chimney and returned to the kitchen. There he placed the porridge pot on the fire, seated himself comfortably next to it, and with great care tied Elsa's rope securely to his leg. What a clever fellow I am, thought Hans; now I can tend the porridge and mind the cow at the same time. Gertrude would never have thought of such an idea. He smiled.

But as fate would have it, it was not long before Elsa grazed a little too close to the edge of the roof and fell off.

Hans, in turn, was dragged by the rope into the fireplace and up the chimney, where he stuck fast. It was not long before the smell of burning porridge reached his upturned nose.

When Gertrude arrived home after a long day in the fields, she saw Elsa dangling from the side of the house. Immediately, she took her scythe and cut the bewildered creature down.

Of course, just as Elsa was released, so too was Hans. And when Gertrude entered the house, she was greeted by an unusually quiet husband. For there was Hans, head first, in the porridge.

"Oh, Hans!" Gertrude cried, and she started to help him out of the pot. As Gertrude cleaned the porridge from Hans's hair with her kerchief, he recounted the misfortunes of his day. When he had finished, Gertrude smiled.

"All is not lost, Hans," she said, "for I had churned a fresh batch of butter yesterday and baked several loaves of bread as well. You see, there is still plenty. But supper may be a little late." Gertrude laughed. "And tomorrow you shall return to the fields, for I could not stand another day like this."

"Yes," Hans croaked. "I knew the fields would prove too much for you."